A Trip to the Circus

By Christine Economos
Illustrated by Lane Gregory

Copyright © 2000 Metropolitan Teaching and Learning Company.
Published by Metropolitan Teaching and Learning Company.
Printed in the United States of America.

ISBN 1-58120-056-0

2 3 4 5 6 7 8 9 CL 03 02 01 00

"This note is from my teacher, Mrs. Baker," said Tasha. "What does it say, Ben?"

"It says that the circus is coming," said Ben. "All the children in your class will go. That's a nice surprise. You'll have a lot of fun there."

"I have never been to the circus," said Tasha. "Have you?"

"I went to the circus once," said Ben. "It was a present from Mom and Pop. I wish I could go a second time. You'll like it, Tasha."

"That was a nice present," said Tasha. "But tell me about the circus. What was it like?"

"There are clowns," said Ben. "They'll make you laugh. There are animals that do tricks. There are people who do tricks, too."

3

"What tricks do they do?" asked Tasha.

"There are animals that ride little bicycles around the ring," said Ben. "There's a dog that can hold a bat with its paws. There are people who do tricks with ropes and balls."

"I wish I could go to the circus now," said Tasha. "How long until we go, Ben?"

"There are still a few days until you go," said Ben. "It says here that a mother or dad can go, too. Maybe Mom or Pop will go."

"That would be a nice present for Mom or Pop," said Tasha. "They would like the circus. But a few days is a long time away. I wish we could go now."

"It's only a few days until we go to the circus," said Mrs. Baker. "I'll tell you about what we'll see. We'll see a lot of clowns."

"The clowns will make all the children laugh," said Tasha. "Ben told me so."

6

"There are other people who will do tricks," said Mrs. Baker.

"They'll do tricks on bicycles," said Tasha. "Dogs will do tricks, too."

"You know a lot about the circus, Tasha," said Mrs. Baker. "Have you been to the circus before?"

"No," said Tasha. "Ben went once. He told me all about it. I hope my mother will come. I think that would be nice."

"Mom," said Tasha. "Mrs. Baker gave me this note to give to you. Maybe it's about our trip to the circus. It's just two days away."

"Tasha, the note says you won't stop talking about the circus," said Mom. "It says you talk about the circus all day long. Mrs. Baker would like you to stop talking about the circus until we go. Do you think you can wait, Tasha? It's very soon. You do talk about the circus a little too much."

"I'll try," said Tasha. "I hope the time goes fast. I want to see the clowns. I want to see what animal I'll like the best. I want to see the little dog that can hold a bat with its paws."

"I want to thank all the mothers and dads who came with their children," said Mrs. Baker. "This is a big day. It's circus day. I know we'll all have a great time. Let's all line up. Then off we'll go to the circus."

"Do you have your things, Tasha?" asked Mom.

"I brought a circus hat, my clown pen, and my snack," said Tasha. "I'm all set. But I don't have a circus toy. Can I get a circus toy when we get there?"

"We aren't going to the circus to get toys," said Mom. "We're going to see animals, clowns, and people doing tricks. We're going to the circus to laugh. Maybe you can get a little toy. We'll see what they have."

"Look, Mom!" said Tasha. "Look at all the colors! Look at all the clowns in the center ring. This circus is the best."

"Now the dogs are going around the center ring," said Mom. "They'll do tricks for us. Look. That's the dog Ben told you about. It's holding a bat in its paws. That's some trick. The other dog can hit a ball with its paw."

"That black dog walks on two legs and pushes a wagon," said Tasha. "Mop can't do that."

"What other tricks will we see in the center ring now?" asked Mom. "There are people on bicycles. Can you see? Tasha? Wake up! This Is no lime To sleep. You'll miss the circus. You don't want to do that. Wake up!"

"Well, you're back!" said Ben. "How was the circus? I bet you laughed a lot. So? How was it?"

"I don't know," said Tasha. "I didn't see the circus. I just saw the dogs doing one or two tricks. That's all."

"You went to the circus, right?" asked Ben. "How come you only saw the dogs?"

"Tasha took a long nap," said Mom. "She missed a lot of the circus."

"Why did you go to sleep?" asked Ben.

"For days all I did was talk about the circus," said Tasha. "But once I got to the circus, I needed to sleep. I trled not to sleep, but I couldn't help it. I missed it all!"

"Well, Tasha," said Ben. "I'm glad you took a nap. Now I hope Mom and Pop will want to take us both to the circus."

"Then you could see the circus a second time," said Tasha. "It would be my second trip to the circus, but my first time seeing it!"